For grandparents- you are golden

~ a.t.

For all our special Nonno's, Farfar's and Grandpa's

~ d.p.

Otto Product Design, Elk Grove, CA USA
Visit us at OttoPD.com

Over in My City:
San Francisco

written by
Anthony Tong

pictures by
Diane Perruzzi

Over in my city in the foggy morning sun,

Was a tall mama seagull and her little seagull one.

"Stretch," said the mama. "I stretch," said the one.

And she stood and she stretched in the foggy morning sun.

2

Over in my city in a park cold and cool,

Was a big mama bison and her little bison two.

"Moo," said the mama. "We moo," said the two.

And they moseyed and they mooed in the park cold and cool.

Over in my city on a pier to the sea,

Was a mama sea lion and her little lions three.

"Clap," said the mama. "We clap," said the three.

And they waddled and they clapped on the pier to the sea.

4

Over in my city by a busy busy store,

Was a mama bumble bee and her little bees four.

"Buzz," said the mama. "We buzz," said the four.

And they beat and they buzzed by the busy busy store.

$0.80/lb

$0.79/lb.

HUMAN

5

Over in my city as the fans come alive,

Was a gray mama pigeon and her little pigeons five.

"Peck," said the mama. "We peck," said the five.

And they poked and they pecked as the fans came alive.

Over in my city through the brambles and the sticks,

Was a happy mama duck and her little duckies six.

"Duck!" said the mama. "We duck," said the six.

And they quacked and they ducked through the brambles and the sticks.

Over in my city where the cars are all driven,

Was a kind mama teacher and her little friends seven.

"Zig," said the mama.

"We zig," said the seven.

And they zigged and they zagged

where the cars are all driven.

8

Over in my city by the great Golden Gate,

Was a blue mama tuna and her little tuna eight.

"Zoom," said the mama. "We zoom," said the eight.

And they zipped and they zoomed by the great Golden Gate.

9

Over in my city above a cable car line,

Was a bright mama bird and her little birdies nine.

"Sing," said the mama. "We sing," said the nine.

And they chirped and they sang above the cable car line.

10

Over in my city in the quiet Lands End,

Was a brown mama squirrel and her little squirrels ten.

"Sleep," said the mama. "We sleep," said the ten.

And they snuggled and they slept in the quiet Lands End.

About the Author

Anthony Tong is a proud father of three growing children.
He loved living in the Inner Sunset, right next to Golden Gate Park.

About the Illustrator

Diane Perruzzi is a freelance illustrator living in northern California.
Her absolutely most favorite city is San Francisco.

See Anthony and Diane's earlier publication, *Over On My Island: Hawaii.*

Made in the USA
Columbia, SC
09 August 2021